The Rat That Ate Poodles

HeebieJeebies
#1

The Rat That Ate Poodles

Paul Buchanan

Created by Paul Buchanan and Rod Randall

Broadman & Holman Publishers
Nashville, Tennessee

0-8054-0170-9

Published by Broadman & Holman Publishers,
Nashville, Tennessee
Acquisitions Editor: Vicki Crumpton
Page Composition: SL Editorial Services

Dewey Decimal Classification: F
Subject Heading: FICTION—JUVENILE/FICTION—CHRISTIAN LIFE/HORROR STORIES
Library of Congress Card Catalog Number: 98-13937

Library of Congress Cataloging-in-Publication Data

Buchanan, Paul, 1959–
The rat that ate poodles / Paul Buchanan
p. cm. — (Heebie Jeebies series ; v. 1)
Summary: Daniel is afraid he has created a giant mutant rat, but his neighbor Brad thinks maybe his guilty conscience is involved, and tries to convince Daniel to let God help him get rid of the rat.
ISBN 0-8054-0170-9 (pbk.)
[1. Rats—Fiction. 2. Christian Life—Fiction. 3. Horror stories.]
I. Title. II. Series
PZ7.B87717Rat 1998
[Fic]—dc21

98-13937
CIP
AC

1 2 3 4 5 02 01 00 99 98

Dedication

For the Sargent Kids

CHAPTER 1

It was a warm night—so warm that I lay on top of my covers wearing my lightweight pajamas. A small electric fan spun silently on my dresser, turning its face this way and that. I looked over at the radio alarm clock on my nightstand. The glowing blue numbers read 2:43.

A dog barked somewhere in the distance and then growled.

I hadn't had a minute of sleep all night. I'd been tossing and turning for hours. It wasn't just the heat, either. I was worried sick about the vicious, hungry creature prowling through my dark neighborhood. I was the only one who knew about it.

That's because *I* was responsible.

It was true. A monster was on the loose out there, and it was my fault.

I held my breath and strained to hear any sounds coming from down in the yard.

My room was awash with dark shadows. Moonlight lit my window. A light breeze made the curtains billow out at me. I heard a dog yelp and whine somewhere out in my neighborhood. Then silence. I stared at the ceiling. Another neighborhood dog gone—and I was to blame. *When would it end?*

I rolled over to the edge of the bed and sat up. I took a deep breath to steady my nerves and crept to the window. I pulled back the curtains and peered down into my shadowy backyard. My heart was pounding. I pressed my forehead against the window screen and felt the warm breeze on my face.

Then I saw it. My stomach churned suddenly. I watched the monster crawl along the dark back wall at the far end of my yard and disappear behind my clubhouse. A *giant, mutant rat*—at least four feet long from the tip of its twitching nose to the end of its hairless pink tail! It was growing bigger every time I saw it. And it was growing fast. It was growing on a steady diet of poodles and Chihuahuas—and maybe a few sleeping cats.

Worst of all, I, Daniel Everett Larkin, had created this monster!

Despite the heat, I pulled my window closed and latched it tight. I switched on my nightstand lamp with shaking fingers. It was clear I'd get no sleep tonight. For a while I just sat there on the edge of my bed wringing my hands. I had to think of a way to stop this monster.

It was hard to believe this whole thing started just last Sunday morning when Dad gave me my summer chore for the week.

CHAPTER 2

Every Sunday since school let out for summer, my dad gave me a new chore every week—weeding Mom's flower beds, cleaning out the rain gutters, or washing and vacuuming all the cars. In other words, all the stuff Mom and Dad could never get to.

This week I had the hardest job of all: clean out the garage. The faded and neglected building stood in the backyard at the end of the driveway, separated from the house. No one had cleaned the garage for as long as I could remember. Some of the junk in there probably hadn't seen the light of day since before I was born, twelve years ago.

"Your job won't be done until we can park both cars in here and shut the door," Dad told me. He squatted like a weight lifter, grunted, and then lifted up the old garage door. Its rusty springs groaned.

When the door was open all the way, Dad dusted off his hands.

I looked inside. The junk was piled so high and tight I couldn't see past the front layer. There were boxes balanced up on the rafters and old dining room chairs turned upside down on the tops of dusty crates. A moldy old rug was rolled up and propped against one wall. A rusty lawn mower stood covered in cobwebs. A gray film of dust covered everything. The place was so crammed full of junk it looked ready to explode. Where in the world did all this stuff come from?

I ran a finger across the top of a cardboard box. The dust seemed as thick as fireplace ash.

"Uh, Dad," I said, studying the dust on my finger. "One week? Unless you're going to rent me a bulldozer, I don't think this is possible."

Dad looked at the garage crammed with junk. It didn't seem to impress him. He got that smile on his face that told me he was about to dust off one of his when-I-was-your-age stories. I thought I'd better say something quick before he got the chance to start.

"At least tell Andrea she has to help me," I said. "She never has to do anything around here."

"Andrea has a job too," Dad told me. "When you bring the junk out of the garage, she'll decide whether it goes to the dump or gets saved for the garage sale."

"Garage sale?"

"On Saturday," Dad said. "Andrea's already making the signs to hang up all over the neighborhood."

Figures she'd *get the easy job,* I thought. She was only nine, but she had plenty of muscle. She could help if she wanted to. But no, not Andrea. She always got to do the fun stuff. Andrea got all the breaks.

I looked at the garage again and sighed. I imagined the hours of back-breaking labor in store for me. I was feeling pretty sorry for myself.

"And I want you to be careful, Daniel," Dad warned me. "I'm sure there are plenty of valuable things in there. If you break anything you'll have to pay for it." He looked down at me with one eyebrow raised, the way he did when he wanted to make sure I was really listening. "I really mean that," he said. "What you break you have to pay for."

Just then I heard something scratching in the back of the garage. Then it fell silent. I stepped closer to the open garage and peered deep into the dusty shadows. The scratching noise started up again.

"You hear that?" I said. "There's some kind of wild animal in there. This could be dangerous."

Dad laughed. "Just a mouse or a rat," he said. "Nothing to worry about. Why when *I* was your age—"

"You had to keep the wolves at bay with a flaming torch?" I guessed.

Dad laughed and mussed my hair. I'd lucked out. I think he forgot what he was going to say. He just stood there and stared at the garage a moment. Then he glanced at his wristwatch and turned to go back in the house.

"By Saturday," he said over his shoulder at me. "Both cars side by side with the door closed. That's your job, Daniel. Don't let me down."

When Dad went inside, I heard my neighbor's kitchen door open, and the family came out to get in their minivan. One of the two boys, Brad, is a year older than I am.

They were all wearing their nicest clothes, and were carrying Bibles. Mr. Tompkin stopped to lock the kitchen door and Mrs. Tompkin slid open the side door of the van.

"Brad," I called.

Brad said something to his mom and came over to the fence. The fence comes up to my chin, but Brad is an inch or two taller than I am. He peered over the top and grinned at me.

"You guys going to church?" I asked, even though I knew they were.

"Yep," Brad said.

"Your parents make you go every Sunday?" I asked.

"They don't *make* me go," Brad said. "I *like* to go."

Brad's dad started up the minivan. He was watching the two of us talk.

"I actually wish I was going with you today," I said.

"You can come with us any time," Brad said. "Why don't you ask your dad?"

"*He's* the reason I wish I was going," I said. "He's making me clean out the garage." I nodded in the direction of the open garage door. "Will you look at what I'm up against?"

Brad looked over at the garage. He shook his head and whistled.

"Man," he said. "Where'd you guys get all that junk?"

"Beats me," I said. "But even *Sunday school* would be better than cleaning up that mess."

"Of course it would," Brad told me, smiling. "Sunday school's pretty cool. You should give it a try sometime."

Brad was always saying stuff like that. It was weird. He was this clean-cut, Sunday school type, but everyone at school still thought he was pretty cool. He was good at hockey and baseball, and he was really funny—somehow Sunday school hadn't turned him into a geek.

Brad's dad beeped the horn.

"Gotta go," Brad said. "We're running late this morning." He turned to go get in the van.

"You think you can come over after lunch and help?" I called after him. "It might actually be kind of fun if there were two of us."

Brad glanced back at the garage again and laughed. "Yeah, OK," he said. "Looks like you're going to need all the help you can get."

CHAPTER 3

After Brad left, I began dragging things out of the garage. I rolled the bikes out first on their flat tires and then dragged out the rusty lawn mower. I moved a few more cardboard boxes and found an old wrought-iron parrot cage. *When did we ever have a parrot?* Every time I moved something, it raised a cloud of dust, and pretty soon everything started to smell like a used book store. I kept feeling like there were cobwebs all over me. I wanted to go inside and wash my hands.

After nearly an hour, I'd only managed to pull out the junk in the very front of the garage, and already the driveway was getting crowded. Besides a dozen cardboard boxes or so, I'd unearthed an ironing board, a broken microwave oven, some old picture frames, an outboard motor, three canoe paddles, and a piano stool. I couldn't imagine anyone wanting to buy *this* junk at a garage sale.

I found a couple of tangled fishing rods wedged between some heavy boxes and tried to pull them out. The rods were caught on something, so I gave them a good yank to get them free. The boxes moved a little, and I heard the scratching noise again way back behind the junk.

I knew it was just a mouse or something, but it still gave me the heebie-jeebies knowing there was something alive in there.

I hadn't been working much longer when I came across something that looked like a green metal briefcase. It was jammed between a stereo speaker and the side wall of the garage. I grabbed it by the handle and pulled it loose. It made a clinking noise, as though full of glass marbles.

I took it out to the middle of the driveway, where there was still an empty space, and set it down flat on the concrete. I wiped some of the dust off the top, but nothing was written there; it was just a plain metal case. I bent the rusty latch down with my thumb and pried the top open. With a rusty groan it opened suddenly.

The case was full of tiny brown bottles, test tubes, and glass beakers. They glimmered in the sun—probably the first light they'd seen in fifteen years. I picked up one of the little bottles and shook it. It sounded half-full of sand. I shook a few more. They had liquid in them. I read the labels. They had big words printed on them, like "potassium chloride" or "silver nitrate." It was an old chemistry set. I'd seen them in stores before but could never afford to buy one. This one was bigger than any I'd seen. It must have been worth around a hundred dollars.

Cool, I thought. *This is not going in any garage sale. This is going under my bed! How hard could it be to invent a stink bomb for Andrea's next slumber party?*

I decided to hide the chemistry set in the backyard clubhouse and then sneak it up to my room later when no one was around. I looked over my shoulder at the house to make sure no one was watching. No one was.

I put all the little bottles back in place and closed the metal lid. I clicked the latch shut, but when I lifted the box by its handle, the lid fell open. All the little bottles, the test tubes, and beakers spilled out in an avalanche of glass. About half of the bottles smashed on the concrete driveway. There was broken glass everywhere!

If Dad saw this I'd owe him a bundle. I'd only been working about an hour and already I'd broken something valuable.

I glanced around to see if anyone had seen me or had heard the noise. No one was around. The kitchen door was still closed.

The powders and liquids from the chemistry set were all running together now amid the broken glass. They began foaming and steaming. Fingers of thick liquid spread out in all directions. After a few seconds, the whole mess turned into a greenish-brownish, bubbling goop.

I knew I was in big trouble with Dad already—but if Mom saw this mess, I'd get it from her too! I had to clean it up—and fast!

I ran inside for a mop and a bucket. I got a broom and dustpan for all the broken glass, trying to make as little commotion as possible so no one would come see what had happened.

I was coming out the kitchen door trying to carry everything when I stopped dead in my tracks. I dropped the broom. It clattered down the back steps. There at the edge of the bubbling green ooze and bits of broken glass was a small, brown rat. He was sniffing and nibbling at the goop, which looked like it was beginning to harden.

It was just a skinny little rat. Nothing to worry about. We'd had one like it in a cage in my sixth-grade classroom. But to be honest, those things have always given me the creeps.

I stood on the back step, frozen, wondering what to do. I had to clean up the mess before Dad or Mom saw it, and I knew the rat was probably more scared of me than I was of it—I could easily scare it away with the broom.

But I suddenly imagined it running at me. Those things are fast. And I imagined the rat scampering up my leg, inside my jeans. I shivered. *Yuck!* The thought of it paralyzed me where I stood.

I pulled the kitchen door closed behind me and just stood on the back step, watching. The skinny rat scampered in a circle around the goop, nibbling here and there, like it was starving. Its nose twitched and it made high-pitched squeaking noises like a hinge that needed oil. Its tiny feet scrabbled around on the concrete driveway. I stooped over slowly and picked up the broom without taking my eyes off the rat.

I heard Mom inside the house moving around and humming to herself. She could come bursting through the back door at any moment. I took a deep breath. I summoned all my courage. I stepped down onto the driveway, holding the broom in front of me like a hockey stick.

I was sure the rat would take off running the minute it saw me coming—but it didn't. It just kept nibbling greedily and looking over to see where I was. It didn't want to stop eating the goop, which must have tasted like candy or something.

I inched closer and closer, holding my breath. I figured that at any second the little rat would streak off into Mom's flower bed, and I'd never see it again. No such luck.

As I edged closer, I reached out with the broom. When the broom came near it, the rat turned and made a weird hissing noise at me. I jumped back. I could feel my heart thumping in my chest. The rat was tiny, but it was mean. It went back to eating the goop like I wasn't there.

This is stupid, I told myself. *It's a little, skinny rat. Why am I so scared?*

I took a few steps closer and jabbed at the rat with the broom.

The rat tumbled backward and then flipped back onto its feet. It raised up on its hind legs and hissed at me again. That got me mad. I jabbed at it again with the broom, harder this time, and the rat streaked up the driveway into the dark garage.

Great, I thought. *I've got to clean out the garage, and that rat could be under any box I lift*. I shivered again and then looked down at the hardening goop at my feet.

I got the mop and broom and went to work on the mess I'd made.

CHAPTER 4

When Brad came over after lunch, there was just a faint green splotch left on the driveway where the goop had been. I'd cleaned it up pretty well—with a little help from the rat. Mom and Dad would never notice.

I didn't tell Brad about the chemistry set. I didn't tell him about the rat either. He was better off not knowing.

I was better off too. I figured I'd send Brad into the garage to get things. *I* was too creeped out. I didn't want to come face to face with the rat again. The thing was already mad at me for swatting it with a broom. It didn't have a grudge against Brad.

"How was church?" I asked Brad as he carried a box of old Ping-Pong paddles out of the garage.

"Great," he said. "We learned about Cain."

"The guy on *Kung Fu?*"

"No." Brad laughed and shook his head. "The guy in the Bible. He got jealous and killed his brother Abel, and then he tried to hide his sin." Brad set the box he was carrying on an old coffee table and slapped the dust from his hands. "Cain could fool everybody else," Brad said, "but there was no way he could hide anything from God."

I looked down at the green splotch on the driveway and swallowed hard. "It's not like God can see everyone *all* the time," I said, feeling a little nervous. "He's got to take a coffee break sometime."

Brad didn't laugh. He stepped back into the garage, picked up an old lampshade, and brushed off some cobwebs. He looked serious.

"God is everywhere," Brad said, bringing the lampshade out into the light. "He sees everything. He knows everything. The Bible says he knows how many hairs are on your head right now."

My head suddenly felt itchy. This conversation was making me more than a little nervous.

"Nothing can be hidden from God," Brad went on. He was looking down at the ground while he spoke. I wondered if he was looking at the stain on the driveway. I wondered if he knew somehow about what I'd done.

"Stop it," I said. "You're giving me the creeps."

Brad laughed and looked up at me. "That's a bad sign, Daniel." he said, still smiling. "You must have a guilty conscience. I always feel *good* knowing that God is everywhere. I never feel alone or forgotten."

He set the lampshade down in the middle of the green stain, turned and went back into the garage for another box. I lifted the lampshade and replaced it with a heavy box of pots and pans. The stain was hidden.

Brad was right. I *did* have a guilty conscience.

An hour later I could see beads of sweat on Brad's forehead. I looked around at the driveway. He'd already moved twice as much junk as I had when I was working on my own. I never saw him take a break. I couldn't believe how hard he was going at it, and I wasn't even paying him.

I had started to unpack a box of eight-track tapes when I noticed Andrea sitting on the back step. She was watching Brad rummage around in the garage with a dopey look on her face. She's had a crush on Brad since she was born, I think. I went over to where she was sitting.

"Don't just sit there," I told her. "Help out."

"Dad said my job was to run the garage sale," she answered, though she was looking at Brad as she spoke. "It's because I'm so good at math," she said loudly at Brad's back.

Brad looked back at her from the garage. He smiled and waved and then started trying to yank a tangled Hula-Hoop free. Andrea pulled her knees up to her chin and hugged her legs. She still had that sappy lovesick look on her face.

"Yeah," I told her, "and you read on a sixth-grade level. Nobody cares."

"*I* care," Brad said from the garage. "I think that's very impressive."

"Aw, don't encourage her," I told him. "It's like feeding a stray cat. She'll hang around us all day."

Brad came out of the garage holding a small cardboard box.

"Hey, this must be mine," he said.

Andrea started laughing hysterically.

"What's so funny?" I asked.

Brad lifted the box higher so I'd see what was written on the side:

BRADS
PAPER CLIPS
STAPLES

Andrea was still cackling on the back step like a crazy woman.

"It's not *that* funny," I told her, not loud enough for Brad to hear.

Brad set down the box and went back in the garage.

Andrea stuck her tongue out at me.

"Grow up," I told her. "You're such a spaz."

Just then Brad let out a yell and jumped back. Then he started laughing.

Andrea jumped up and ran to the garage. She stood in the doorway and peered inside. I was right behind her.

Brad just stood there laughing. He had one hand on his chest like he'd just had a heart attack or something.

"What happened?" Andrea asked wide eyed. "Are you OK?"

I didn't say anything. I already *knew* what had scared Brad.

It took a minute for Brad to stop laughing and catch his breath.

"Nothing," he said at last. "It was a rat. It was just a big rat."

"Wait a minute," I said. "You saw a *big* rat?"

"Yeah," he said. "A big *fat* one. About this big." He held his fingers about a foot apart.

I felt a chill go through me. *Another rat?* I thought. But something inside me told me the situation was far worse.

CHAPTER 5

It was close to midnight. Mrs. Petersen's black poodle, Truman, had been barking for nearly an hour.

Mrs. Petersen's house was right behind ours. She lived by herself. Truman was her only companion—so no one ever tried to make her get rid of the dog. But sometimes it yapped all night and kept everyone in the neighborhood awake.

I rolled on my side and pressed my pillow on top of my head, trying to squeeze out the noise, but I could still hear the barking. I was getting angry.

I know it wasn't really the dog's fault. I was having trouble getting to sleep for other reasons. I felt bad about all the stuff I'd done that day. I'd broken the chemistry set and hid it from Dad. I'd made Brad do most of the work in the garage, when it was supposed to be *my* chore. And on top of all that, I'd been mean to Andrea again. It's hard to sleep when you have a guilty conscience.

So now I was tossing and turning in bed, listening to Truman the poodle barking down in Mrs. Petersen's yard. I suppose I deserved it, but I was angry anyway.

I sat up on the edge of the bed.

"Woof, woof, woof," Truman barked.

I got up and went over to the window. I was going to yell down at Truman—I knew it would only make him bark louder, but I was angry. I thought if I yelled at the dog it might make me feel better.

I slid open the window and pressed my forehead against the screen. Truman stopped barking suddenly. I squinted out into the night trying to see him in his backyard. I wanted to throw something at him.

There was only a sliver of moon in the sky. It was pretty dark. I couldn't see much of anything.

I waited. There was no more barking, just crickets chirping softly down in the darkness. Maybe Truman had tired of barking and fallen asleep.

Finally! I thought. I sighed and rolled back into bed.

As soon as my head hit the pillow, Truman began barking again—louder and wilder than ever.

He was growling and yelping and barking all at once. He sounded like he was going crazy.

He was driving *me* crazy.

I jumped out of bed and went to the window. I was about to shout, when something caught me off guard. I saw a big, dark shape move slowly along the top of the wall that separated Truman's yard from our own. I couldn't make out what the thing was, and then it suddenly stopped moving.

I pressed my nose closer to the screen and squinted down into the darkness. I could feel the dust on the window ledge under my fingers. I felt the damp night air on my face. I smelled freshly cut grass from someone's yard. I peered down at the wall.

The thing moved again. I held myself still.

I stared at it. I could just make it out in the shadows: a giant rat, dragging its long, bare tail behind it! It was at least four feet long!

My mouth dropped open. My knees went weak. I couldn't breathe. I stumbled back and sat on the edge of my bed, stunned.

When I went back to the window the thing was gone, and Truman had stopped barking.

A giant rat? It was impossible—but I'd seen it with my own eyes. I pinched my arm. *Youch!* I was definitely awake. This was no dream.

I sat on my bed again and fit the pieces together in my mind: the skinny rat from the garage, the bubbling green ooze, the fat rat that Brad saw. I got a horrible sinking feeling as the realization hit me: *I had created a monster.*

The next morning Mom shook me awake. I yawned and glanced over at my radio alarm clock. It was after ten. The radio on the clock was playing rock music softly. I'd slept right through it.

"You looked so peaceful, I didn't have the heart to wake you up," she told me, sitting on the edge of my bed.

Peaceful? I thought, rubbing my eyes. *That's the* last *thing I'm feeling!*

"Come on down, and I'll make you breakfast," Mom said. "Everyone else has already eaten." She leaned over and kissed me on the forehead, then left the room, closing the door behind her.

I got up and got dressed, but my mind wasn't on what I was doing. I was still thinking about the giant, mutant rat. I was about to pull on my tennis shoes when I noticed I was wearing one brown sock and one white one.

I am losing my mind, I told myself.

I sat down on my bed and tried to relax. I folded my hands on my lap. I straightened my back. I took a few deep breaths. From where I sat I could see my face in my dresser mirror. My hair was sticking up on one side.

It must have been some kind of dream, I explained to myself. It *had* to be a dream. Things like this don't happen in real life. You can't make a rat grow four feet long with a chemistry set. I was almost wide awake now, and I was beginning to see things more clearly. Things were beginning to make more sense.

How lame can you get? I'd let myself get all worked up over some dumb nightmare. I smiled at my reflection and shook my head. *You dummy,* I thought. *You big, dumb knucklehead.*

It was kind of funny when you thought about it in the cold light of day. Of *course* it had been a dream. Sometimes dreams can seem so real. Sometimes your imagination can run away with you.

I got up and went to the open window chuckling at myself. How could I be so silly?

I looked out through the screen window, down into the yard. Everything was green and pretty in the morning sun. Some of Mom's flowers were blooming red and blue. Birds were singing.

My little clubhouse looked shady and cool under the sycamore tree. The lawn was a rich shade of green. All the boxes of junk were arranged neatly on the driveway. I could even see Mrs. Petersen on her back step calling for Truman over and over again. Everything was as it should be. I stretched and took a deep, relaxing breath.

It was then that I noticed the row of fresh fingerprints in the thick dust on the window sill where I'd stood looking out last night.

I stumbled back and sat down on the edge of the bed.

It was no dream!

CHAPTER 6

I didn't go out in the backyard that morning until Brad came knocking on our front door after I'd eaten breakfast. I was just too scared. I was still sitting at the breakfast table when the doorbell rang.

"What's up?" Brad said when I opened the front door. "I thought we were going to get to work bright and early."

"I overslept," I told him as we headed through the house toward the back kitchen door. "Old Truman kept me awake all night with his barking."

"Oh yeah?" Brad said. "I must have slept right through it."

I opened the back kitchen door and stood back so Brad could go first—I was *that* scared!

I followed Brad down the steps and into the yard like a shadow. I walked as close behind him as I could. I was looking around all over the place as if something might jump out on me from anywhere. Brad stopped outside the garage, and I ran into him.

Brad laughed. "What is the matter with you, Daniel?" he asked me. "You act like there's a tiger loose out here."

I tried to laugh casually at his joke, but the noise I made didn't sound right to me. I was too nervous. I was tongue-tied. I couldn't think of anything to say. "I'm worthless till I've had my coffee," I blurted out. It was something Dad liked to say.

Brad looked at me a few seconds and then laughed again, shaking his head. I felt like an idiot. Brad went into the garage and dragged out a dusty old dresser with a cracked mirror. He knelt down and started going through the drawers.

I watched him for a few minutes as he worked hard in the bright morning sun. He smiled and hummed to himself as he worked. It was hard not to envy him. He didn't seem to have a worry in the world.

The closer it got to lunch time, the more I relaxed. Nothing had happened all morning. I even went in the garage a few times. *Hadn't I read somewhere that rats usually sleep during the day and only come out at night?* Still, I held my breath every time I lifted a box or moved a piece of furniture—just in case there was something behind it.

Andrea told us what to load onto Dad's pickup for the dump. The rest of the stuff she arranged on the lawn and driveway. She dusted things off or washed them with a bucket of soapy water, getting them ready for the garage sale. She carried a clipboard and kept writing things on it with a pencil she kept tucked behind her ear. Every few minutes she'd look over to see what Brad was doing.

"He's four years older than you, Andrea," I told her, setting a box of old LP records down on the lawn in front of her. "He'd fall in love with Truman the poodle before he'd give *you* a second look."

"Four years isn't so much," she said flipping through the records and pulling some out to save for the garage sale.

"Not so much?" I said. "Are you kidding? He's like *twice* as old as you."

"He's *forty-four percent* older," she said, closing the box of records. "And it doesn't make any difference."

I stared at her, blinking for a second. "Forty-four percent?" I said. "You figured that out in your head? You're one weird kid, Andrea."

She ignored me. "Dad's *six* years older than Mom," she reminded me. "It doesn't make any difference."

"Yeah, but they're old," I pointed out. "A thirteen-year-old guy is *not* going to be interested in a nine-year-old twerp like you."

She stood up and kicked the half-full box of records. "These go in the truck," she said and stomped off into the house.

Around noon, Andrea came out the kitchen door carrying a tray covered with a linen napkin. She was wearing a white frilly dress and a straw hat with cloth flowers on it. She walked by Brad and me like a movie star and headed across the lawn. "We'll be dining in the clubhouse," she said as she passed.

I looked over at Brad. He was smiling. He set down the shoeshine kit he was holding and followed Andrea into the clubhouse. I felt myself blush. I stood there a moment wishing I were an only child, and then I followed Brad and Andrea into the clubhouse.

Dad built this clubhouse before Andrea was even born, but it still smelled like sawdust inside. I didn't go in there much anymore, except when I wanted to play darts.

It wasn't tall enough for Brad or me to stand up straight—only Andrea could. She pulled three small chairs up to the low table and made us sit down. She made sure she was sitting next to Brad, of course. I thought I was going to die of embarrassment.

Andrea served us peanut butter and jelly sandwiches sliced into triangles with the crusts cut off. She poured us orange juice from Mom's crystal decanter and drank her glass with her pinkie sticking out. She kept calling us "gentlemen." I wanted to strangle her.

I thought someone as cool as Brad would bust out laughing and run home, but he didn't. He even played along with her, calling her "Miss Andrea." It actually turned out to be kind of fun once I started to relax.

Watching Brad made me realize how mean I was to Andrea. She was just a little kid after all—I shouldn't get mad at her so easily. I thought maybe I should play along with her more, the way Brad did.

Andrea put the leftover sandwiches in a Tupperware container so Brad could take them home with him.

After lunch, when we climbed out of the clubhouse, Andrea and Brad went back to the garage, but I went over to look at the back wall. I ran my hand along the top of it, where I'd seen the giant rat crawling the night before. If the monster *did* exist—and I was sure it did!—it had left no marks on the wall.

Remembering what I'd seen the night before tied my stomach in knots. There was no way to know what might happen next. The rat seemed to be growing incredibly fast. At this rate it would be the size of a cow by the time we had our garage sale!

It seemed like I ought to tell someone what had happened—people should be warned. After all, the thing might be dangerous. But if I told Dad or Mom, they'd probably think I was crazy.

And even if they *did* believe me, I'd be in big trouble. I'd been grounded for two weeks once for breaking a clock. I couldn't begin to imagine the punishment for creating a giant, mutant rat. I felt trapped. I felt like banging my head against the wall.

When I returned to the driveway, Brad was already hard at work, and Andrea was loading things on the back of Dad's pickup for the dump. This was *my* chore, and I was the only one not working.

I went into the garage and tried to pull out a rickety old rocking chair. I couldn't budge it at first; one of the runners was caught on something. I clapped the dust off my hands and got a good grip on the back of the chair. I gave it a yank. It suddenly came loose, and a box of kitchen utensils toppled off a high stack of boxes and landed with a clatter amid a cloud of dust.

Just then, I heard something moving in the garage. It was way in the back. It didn't sound like a little rat this time. It was definitely something big. I looked over at Brad. He blew some dust off an old dart board and held it at arm's length, studying it. It seemed like he hadn't even heard the noise.

I looked back at Andrea. She was struggling to close the tailgate on the truck. Had I imagined the sound?

When I picked up the chair, I heard the noise again. It was a scratchy, rustling sound—like coarse fur rubbing against something hollow. Brad still acted like nothing was happening. I peered into the dark reaches of the garage. A tall floor lamp swayed suddenly in the back. My heart pounded. I started to back away from the garage, holding the chair in front of me like a shield. I tried to say something to warn the others, but I couldn't make my mouth work.

Suddenly the thing rushed out of the garage. I just saw a streak of gray fur coming straight at me. I screamed, threw the chair I was holding and ran. I vaulted over the fence into Brad's yard. I never knew I could jump so high. I sprinted halfway across Brad's yard before I looked back. When I did, Andrea and Brad were both watching me, laughing.

"What's got into you today?" Brad asked. "I've never seen anyone so jumpy."

I looked at them for a moment, confused and alarmed. I walked back over to the fence feeling foolish. My heart still thumped in my chest like a frightened rabbit.

When I looked over the fence, Andrea was holding a gray cat, stroking it. She was still laughing. The rocking chair was rocking on its own where it had landed inside the garage.

"It's just Missy, the Jacobs's cat," Andrea said, scratching the cat between its ears. It tilted its head and purred. "She was playing in the garage. Didn't you see her go in?"

CHAPTER 7

I had to be sure. I was tired of being so confused. I had to know if this was really happening or if I was going crazy. I had to find out if there really was a giant, mutant rat prowling the neighborhood or whether it was all in my wild imagination. Whichever way it turned out, it wouldn't be much fun—but at least I'd know for sure.

My plan was to stay awake until Truman started barking. Then I'd sneak down into the backyard with my flashlight and baseball bat and see if this was all in my head. I was terrified, but it was something I knew I had to do.

When I went to bed that night, I kept my jeans and tee shirt on and pulled the covers over me. I hung my Chicago Bulls windbreaker over the chair at my desk and put my flashlight in the pocket. I also made sure it had fresh batteries. I propped my aluminum baseball bat next to my dresser. When I heard Mom and Dad coming up to say good night, I pulled the covers up to my chin.

My door opened quietly, and Dad peeked in. When he saw I was awake, he and Mom came in and stood at the side of my bed.

"You're making some real progress in the garage," Dad said. "You've been doing some good, hard work. I'm proud of you, Daniel. Real proud."

"We didn't even have to tell him to go to bed tonight," Mom said to Dad. "He came up here by himself."

Mom bent over and kissed me on the forehead. I held the covers tightly under my chin.

"My son," she said straightening up. "He's so responsible all of a sudden."

When Mom and Dad closed the bedroom door behind them, I rolled over and switched off my bedside lamp. I lay there in the dark looking at my window and thinking about what Mom had said. I had a creepy, sinking feeling. Mom was right. Maybe I *was* responsible—responsible for creating a monster!

Suddenly I realized I'd been sleeping—I had that bad taste in my mouth. I rolled over and looked at the clock. A quarter to three.

I listened for Truman's barking, but I didn't hear him. In fact I didn't remember hearing him at all that night. *What woke me up, then?* I laid my head back on my pillow and yawned. I was warm and sleepy. It was the middle of the night. Suddenly, going out in the backyard to look for a monster didn't seem like such a hot idea. I just wanted to roll over and go back to sleep.

Then I heard it. It sounded like someone sweeping a rough wooden floor with a broom. I held my breath and listened. Soon there was a scratching noise; then a loud klunk and a tearing noise, coming from the backyard. Now I knew what had wakened me.

I went to the window and looked down into the yard. It was cloudy tonight, so there was no moon to light the yard at all. I couldn't even make out the shape of the clubhouse, it was so dark out there.

I rolled out of bed and pulled on my jacket. I checked in the pocket for my flashlight. I slipped on my shoes and tied the laces. My fingers tingled, and it was hard to make a bow. I felt around in the dark until I found my baseball bat. My mouth felt dry. I opened my bedroom door as quietly as I could and crept downstairs.

I tiptoed past the humming refrigerator and the dripping kitchen faucet. I paused with my hand on the cold kitchen doorknob. It took me a minute to gather up the courage to open the door. I twisted the knob and pulled. The door creaked slowly open, and I felt the night air on my face.

I peered into the dark backyard. With the door open, the commotion sounded much louder. There was a thumping noise and a wheezing. I decided to leave the door open, in case I needed to get back inside fast. I swallowed hard and stepped down onto the back steps, shining the flashlight all around in the darkness. My hand was shaking, so the flashlight's beam did too.

I inched toward the open garage as quietly as I could, stepping over an old record player and shuffling around a bag of rusty golf clubs. There was so much junk arranged in the driveway now, it was hard to move without making noise. I held the baseball bat high in my right hand, ready to club anything that rushed at me.

I froze. The noises had stopped. All I could hear was the chirping of crickets in distant yards. The breeze stirred the hairs on the back of my neck. I shone my light through the open garage door. The shaky beam ran along all the junk stacked up high. Shadows crawled along the walls as I slowly moved the beam of light from one side of the garage to the other. It lit up the rafters full of cobwebs and the swirls of dust in the air. I stood still and listened. I held my breath, waiting.

The noises began again—but they weren't in the garage. They were coming from somewhere in the dark backyard. I threaded my way among the boxes and old furniture and stood on the edge of the back garden. I shone the light around Mom's flower beds. Nothing was moving. My right arm was getting tired from holding the bat aloft, so I switched hands, careful not to drop the flashlight. I stepped over Mom's flower bed onto the lawn.

A loud thump made me jump. I stabbed the light toward the clubhouse door where the noise had come from. The beam lit up two red eyes in the dark. A long, pink tail dangled from the doorway. The beam of light began to shake uncontrollably. I wanted to yell, but I couldn't breathe. I stood there frozen in fear.

The two eyes peered at me from the dark doorway. They looked evil and angry in the shaking light. The giant rat didn't move. It held perfectly still and stared at me coldly from the shadows. My legs felt like rubber. I gripped the baseball bat tightly and slowly stepped backward toward Mom's flower bed and the concrete driveway.

I was inching my way back toward the open kitchen door when the thing snorted at me angrily.

I dropped my flashlight and bat and dashed toward the door, plowing through Mom's flower bed, tripping over boxes and knocking down furniture as I clambered across the driveway cluttered with junk. I heard things clanking and clattering to the ground behind me. It sounded like the rat was right behind me.

I leaped up the back steps to the open kitchen door without looking back. I had no idea how close behind me the monster was. As I slammed the door and twisted the lock, my heart was pounding crazily. I pressed my weight against the door for a few seconds and then sprinted through the kitchen and up the stairs to my room. I jumped into bed and yanked the covers over my head.

In a few minutes I got my breath back—and a little bit of my courage. I crept to my open bedroom window and peered down into the yard. My flashlight lay on the lawn, lighting up a triangle of grass and making it hard to see anything else in the yard.

After a few seconds, the noises began again—a thumping and wheezing in the clubhouse. I closed the window and latched it tight.

I lay on my bed again and stared at the ceiling, trying to think of what to do now that I was sure.

Mom was right; I *was* responsible. I'd created this monster.

Now how was I going to get rid of it?

CHAPTER 8

The next morning, I overslept. The radio on my alarm clock had gone off at eight, and I'd slept right through it again. It was no big surprise; I hadn't had much sleep all week. It was more surprising that I had slept at all, considering what I'd seen last night.

I dragged myself out of bed and tiptoed to the window, half expecting to see the huge rat down in the yard waiting for me. The yard was empty, of course. Everything was as it should be. Everything looked completely normal. To anyone else it would seem like a pleasant summer morning with sunshine and birds, flowers and green lawns. But I knew better.

I got dressed and brushed my teeth, and then I trudged downstairs to see if there was anything left from breakfast. Everyone else had already eaten and the dishes, sticky with pancake syrup, were stacked in the kitchen sink. No one seemed to be home.

Just my luck, I thought, feeling sorry for myself. Everyone else gets Mom's pancakes and *I* have to eat cold cereal.

I got a bowl down from the cupboard and looked in the pantry for the cereal. It was worse than I'd expected—we were all out of Cap'n Crunch; all we had was Mom's healthy cereal. I poured myself half a bowl and went to the refrigerator for the milk, but there was none of that left either. The empty plastic jug was in the recycling bin.

I got a spoon and slumped down at the table. I lifted a dry spoonful of granola to my mouth. It tasted like sawdust. It took a few minutes before I could manage to swallow it, and then it felt like sandpaper going down my throat.

"Ugh," I said out loud. "How could my life get any worse?"

"About *time* you got up," a voice said. It was Andrea. She was coming in the back kitchen door with a big stack of books tucked under her chin. "I thought I was going to have to carry all the books upstairs by myself," she puffed.

"What books?"

"I found a bunch of books in some of the boxes from the garage." She came over and hefted them up on the table top in front of me. She was red-faced and breathing hard. "Mom said I could keep them," she told me. "I need you to carry them up to my room."

"What do you need with more books?" I asked, tilting my head to read some of the titles. "You already have a million of them and you check out a hundred more from the library every week."

"You're just jealous because I can read on—"

"A sixth grade level," I finished the sentence for her. "Yes, I know. And you'll probably graduate from Harvard when you're my age." Andrea made a face, but I ignored her. "So you should be smart enough to realize that there's no way I'm going to lug all those books upstairs for you."

"But they're too heavy for me," she said in her whiniest voice. "I'm just a fourth grader."

"Well it's time you learned to *carry* books on a sixth grade level," I told her.

"Mom said you had to carry them for me," Andrea informed me. "She's afraid I'm going to hurt myself going up the stairs."

"Mom said that?" I asked. "What if *I* get hurt going up the stairs? How come nobody cares about that?"

"You're a boy," Andrea told me.

"What's *that* supposed to mean?"

"It means you're expendable," Andrea said smugly. "Mom's already mad at you for missing breakfast again, so you'd better do it if you know what's good for you."

I sighed and shook my head. Mom never seemed to get mad at Andrea. Life could be so unfair. I stood up.

"You're sure Mom said I had to do this?" I asked.

"Right before she went out grocery shopping."

"Great," I sulked. I stood up and slid the stack of books to the edge of the table, so I could get a good grip on them.

"The rest are out on the driveway," Andrea said.

I groaned. "You mean there's more?"

"We're just getting started," Andrea said grinning. She really seemed to be enjoying herself. I worked my hands under the stack of books and pulled them off the edge of the table. I groaned. They were heavier than I thought they'd be.

I turned and struggled out of the kitchen toward the stairway. Andrea must have noticed the bowl of dry cereal I'd been trying to eat.

"This morning's pancakes were delicious," she called after me from the kitchen.

I pushed Andrea's bedroom door open with my shoulder and looked around for somewhere to put down the stack of books. Her room was full of stuffed toys and frilly things. There were flowers on the wallpaper and posters of kittens. Everything was pink. It was enough to give a guy the creeps.

Andrea had a bookcase over near her desk, but it was already full of books. I looked around for somewhere to put the stack I was holding. I couldn't hold them much longer. I walked over and set them on top of Andrea's desk, which was much clearer than mine ever was.

I shook the kinks out of my arms and glanced down at Andrea's bookcase. It was mostly full of dumb books about girls who had horses or who lived on the prairie a long time ago.

Then I noticed the *Encyclopedia of World Wildlife.* It was a set of slim volumes bound in white. I sat on the floor and pulled out the one that said "Raccoon to Tarsier." I flipped through the pages, looking for "Rat."

The book was filled with pictures and maps, like Dad's *National Geographic* magazines. There were four pages about all the different kinds of rats. It took me a minute to find the picture that looked most like the one I'd seen eating the goop I'd made when I dropped the chemistry set.

In the photo, the rat seemed to be snarling at the camera. Its sharp teeth were bared. Its eyes seemed to smolder with malice. It was the brown rat, also known as the Norway rat, wharf rat, or *Rattus Norvegicus.*

I started reading the article.

> The adult brown rat grows to a length of about seven to ten inches (18 to 26 centimeters), including the tail. The most common species in North America, the brown rat is extremely destructive. It climbs with amazing ease and is able to jump. Its powerful jaws and teeth enable it to chew through wood. It has even been known to bite through lead pipes. These abilities enable the brown rat to reach virtually any source of food. When driven by hunger or thirst, they are unrelenting in their attempts to enter buildings.

I stopped reading and looked over at Andrea's window. It was just like mine. The tiny metal latch that held it shut would be no match for a four-foot rat who could chew through metal and wood. I imagined the thing scrambling up the outside of the house. A shiver went through me.

I went back to reading the article.

> Brown rats thrive in human habitations, often spreading such diseases as the plague,

> typhus fever, rat bite fever, hemorrhagic jaundice, tularemia, rabies, trichinosis, and salmonelosis.

I swallowed hard. I had no idea what those diseases were, but I figured the harder they were to pronounce, the worse they must be.

> Brown rats are nocturnal, and as such have acutely developed senses, especially the senses of hearing and touch. While many varieties of rats are herbivorous, the brown rat is omnivorous. The most aggressive variety of rat, the brown rat frequently attacks poultry, domestic animals, and even humans.

Even humans? I looked at the picture of the rat. It was easy to imagine it being six feet long—or however large the monster rat was by now; I didn't get a good look at it last night. I looked at the inch-long, razor-sharp teeth; the menacing look in his eyes; the sharp claws. I imagined a huge version of the same rat lunging at me.

"Daniel," Andrea called from the doorway. I jumped about a foot off the ground.

"Stop doing that," I shouted wildly. "Stop sneaking up on people."

"No need to bite my head off," she sniffed. "I was only coming to tell you that Brad is here." Andrea made a face and turned to go back down the stairs.

I closed the book and slid it back into its gap in the bookcase.

When Brad and I went out the kitchen door, he went straight to the garage, but I tiptoed over to look at the clubhouse. I must have looked like an idiot, creeping up on the clubhouse door like I half expected it to bite me. I stooped down and peeked in from a few yards away. The clubhouse was empty. I crouched into the doorway and looked inside.

The Tupperware box Andrea had put the extra sandwiches in was clawed and chewed to shreds and scattered all over the plywood floor. The sandwiches were gone.

"Look what I found," Brad said, tapping me on the shoulder.

I jumped half out of my skin and banged my head on the top of the doorway. "Owww," I moaned and turned to him rubbing my head. I hadn't heard him come up behind me.

He was holding the flashlight I'd dropped on the lawn last night. "Are you OK?" he asked as he looked beyond me at the inside of the clubhouse. His mouth dropped open. *"What happened in here?"* he said.

The chairs were lying on their sides. My dart board had been knocked off the wall. Shredded comic books were strewn everywhere. Baseball cards were scattered along the back wall. Curls of torn Tupperware littered the wooden floor and the table.

Brad looked at me. I must have looked pale because he stared at me a long time. "What's going on here?" he asked. "You've got me worried, Daniel. You've been acting weird all week. Are you in some kind of trouble? Is there anything I can do?"

I looked at him, and then I looked past him at the house in the bright morning sunlight and at my own bedroom window.

"I'm OK," I said after a moment. "Everything's fine."

"How come *I* have to help Andrea?" I asked Mom through the station wagon window that afternoon. "She hasn't helped *me* clean out the garage."

"You've had plenty of help," Andrea said smugly from the passenger seat.

Mom started up the engine and adjusted the rearview mirror.

"I don't have time," I pleaded. "I've got tons of stuff to do."

"Just get in the car," Mom told me. "It'll only take a few minutes. Andrea will need help hammering in the stakes."

Right, I thought. As if Andrea the Brainiac couldn't figure out how to use a hammer!

I climbed in the back seat and slammed the car door. I folded my arms and glared at the back of Andrea's head as we backed down the driveway. I was fuming.

Our first stop was at the end of our street. Mom turned the corner and pulled up to the curb. Andrea—who of course got to ride shotgun when Dad wasn't in the car—got out and opened my door. I just sat there with my arms folded.

"The signs are in the back," Andrea said in the extremely polite voice she always used around Mom. "Could you get one please?"

Mom was watching me in the rearview mirror. I could tell by the look in her eyes she was getting mad at me. I sighed and unbuckled my seat belt.

I kneeled on my seat and looked in the back. There was a big stack of neatly painted poster board signs stapled to wooden stakes and Dad's small toolbox. I pulled out one of the signs and grabbed the hammer from the toolbox.

I carried the sign to the curb and picked a spot where the ground looked softer. Andrea stood behind me, supervising.

"More to the left," she nagged. "No, the *other* left."

If Mom hadn't been there, I would have told her a thing or two.

"OK, right there," she said finally.

I pounded in the stake. While I was hammering, I noticed another poster on a stake nearby:

MISSING POODLE
ANSWERS TO "TRUMAN"
$25 REWARD

At the bottom was Mrs. Petersen's address and phone number.

"What's the matter with *you?*" Andrea asked. "You look like you've seen a ghost."

Andrea read Mrs. Petersen's sign over my shoulder.

"Huh," she said. "That's too bad. Mrs. Petersen will sure miss Truman—but I don't think anyone else in the neighborhood will. Maybe we'll all get more sleep now."

Andrea went back to the station wagon and opened the back door for me.

I continued to stare at the poster. I was imagining poor Truman the poodle running across the dark lawn being chased by a huge rat with glowing red eyes. I wondered how big the rat was now. If it was eating poodles it must be huge!

"Come on!" Andrea called from the passenger seat of the station wagon. "We've got about twenty more signs to do."

I shook the image from my head and got in the station wagon. Mom pulled away from the curb. Andrea told Mom about Truman. I didn't say a word.

But Truman wasn't the only victim. There were plenty of others. Every time we passed a corner, there seemed to be another sign about a missing dog or cat. Andrea noticed it too.

"What's happening around here?" she asked. "That's five cats and three dogs missing. There must be a pet burglar loose in the neighborhood."

Mom laughed. She always laughed at Andrea's jokes, no matter how lame they were.

The next corner we drove past had a sign that said *two* Scotch terriers were missing. I had created one hungry monster! My stomach was knotted again. If the monster had eaten ten house pets in just a few days, he must be growing even faster than I'd imagined. He'd be big as a Winnebago in no time!

"Maybe we've got a mountain lion coming around," Andrea said looking out the window. "We'd better be careful."

"Don't be silly," Mom told her. "These signs are always up all over the neighborhood. Pets run away all the time. And most people forget to take down the signs once they get their pets back." We turned back onto our own street. "You're just noticing the signs for the first time because you're putting up signs of your own," Mom told Andrea. "There's nothing to worry about. There's no mountain lion within a hundred miles of here."

I just sat there, silent and miserable, in the back of the station wagon. I knew Mom was half right. There was no mountain lion.

But there was *plenty* to worry about!

CHAPTER 9

That night I lay in bed staring at the ceiling, listening for any noise down in the yard. I wondered where the monster rat was now and where it slept during the day. It couldn't live in the garage anymore; there was no way it could squeeze through its little rat doorway anymore, wherever it was—and I kept the garage door closed when we weren't working on cleaning it out.

Maybe the monster slept under one of the houses on our street, or perhaps it lived in Mr. Jacobs's empty tool shed. I imagined Mr. Jacobs pulling open the door, seeing the red-eyed monster inside, and falling to the ground clutching his chest.

It seemed inevitable. It was only a matter of time before something terrible happened.

Worry gnawed at my stomach. If the monster I

created was hunting down cats and dogs now, how long before it attacked some kid who wandered out after dark? The words in the encyclopedia echoed in my mind: *The brown rat frequently attacks poultry, domestic animals, and even humans.*

I knew I had to do something. But what?

Should I call the police? I imagined dialing 9-1-1. What could I tell them? *Sir,* I imagined myself saying, *I seem to have created a giant, mutant rat that ate my neighbor's poodle. Could you send over a patrol car, please?* No one was going to believe me. If they did send over a car it would be to haul me away to some kind of nut house!

Should I tell Mom and Dad? *Dad,* I imagined myself saying, *could you buy me a mouse trap—one about the size of Mom's station wagon? It's for this monster rat I made last Sunday. It's OK; you can deduct it from my allowance.* Nothing doing. I'd told Mom and Dad so many lies in the past, I knew they'd just ground me.

I rolled over on my side in bed and looked at my bedroom window. I could feel the cool night breeze. I wondered what was going on down in the yard right now.

It felt so lonely being the only one who knew about the monster. It was like a heavy weight on my shoulders. I thought about what Brad had said about God—about how he was always with us. Brad said he never felt alone because he knew that God was always there. I wished *I* felt that way.

I wished I were like Brad in a lot of other ways too. He was always so patient with Andrea; I was always getting mad at her. Being angry all the time is no fun. It's like another kind of weight you have to carry around.

Sometimes I'd see Brad and his dad sitting out on their front porch laughing and talking. It was almost like they were friends. Whenever I was alone with *my* dad, we never seemed to have anything to talk about.

At school I spent all my time trying to impress the cool kids. Brad never seemed to care what the cool kids thought—and yet everyone seemed to think *he* was cool, just because he didn't care about impressing anyone.

I rolled on my back and looked up at the ceiling. OK, I decided, if I'm going to tell anyone about the giant rat, it's got to be Brad. *He* seems to have his act together. Maybe *he'll* know what to do.

When the scraping noise woke me up, I looked over at my alarm clock, which read 1:22 A.M. I'd been asleep a couple of hours. I kept still in bed and listened. I could feel my heart racing in my chest.

When I heard the noise again I blew out the breath I'd been holding and laughed. It wasn't down in the yard. It was just a moth bumping against my window screen. I rolled over on my back and closed my eyes.

I was drifting off to sleep when the noise came again. It was a papery scratching noise—not very loud. I tried to ignore it and go back to sleep.

The scraping noise didn't stop, and now it was getting loud enough to bother me. I looked over at the window screen, but it was too dark to see the moth, so I reached over and switched on the lamp on my nightstand.

When I looked back at the window, two large, red eyes were glaring in at me. My mouth fell open.

I froze and stared back at the beady, glowing eyes. Their gaze bored into me, and I could feel my heart thudding in my chest again.

The rat scowled at me a moment longer and then a sharp claw came out of the darkness and poked through my window screen like the blade of a curved knife. The claw slowly tore down the length of the screen. It sounded like a zipper.

I rolled away from the window and dropped

down on the floor beside my bed on my hands and knees. My legs were tangled and twisted in the bedclothes. I peered over the bed.

The giant rat slid its long twitching nose through the slit in the screen and sniffed at the air of my bedroom. The nose glistened black in the light of my bedside lamp. And the long whiskers, like porcupine quills, cast shadows back on what was left of the window screen.

I quietly kicked myself free of the twisted bedclothes. When I peeked over the edge of the bed at the window again, I saw the rat trying to wedge itself through into my bedroom—its fat, furry body filled the entire window. Its front paws were on the floor now.

My room was suddenly filled with a stench like the inside of a trash can. I glanced around the room for my baseball bat, but then I remembered I'd left it leaning in the corner by the window.

The rat's front paws scrambled and scratched at the wooden floor now, trying to find a way to pull its hindquarters through the too-small window. I heard the wood of the window frame creak and crack.

In my terror, I couldn't think of what to do. I tried to scream, but I couldn't make my mouth work. I pressed myself down on the floor and squeezed my eyes shut. I could feel my heart beating against the floorboards. I hoped the rat wouldn't be able to get inside. I wondered if I should make a run for the door, but just then I heard a loud *whump*, and I knew that the rat was in the room with me now. I scrambled under my bed.

From under the box spring, I could see four pink feet padding around my dresser, their claws clicking on the floor—and I could see the long, pink tail dragging behind. I heard the rat sniffing around my dresser and bookshelf. Books and toys fell to the ground as the rat ransacked my room searching for something to eat. All the while, the rat chattered and squeaked. I was shaking all over, but I tried not to make a sound.

I heard a thump on the floor—then something touched my leg! I gasped and jerked back my leg, banging my knee on the box spring. I looked down at my leg to see what had touched me. It was just a baseball that had rolled under the bed. But it was too late now. The rat had heard me!

The room was silent. I could imagine the rat, its front paws on my dresser, peering around the room now, wondering where the sound had come from, its twitching nose testing the air.

The hairless pink tail wandered under the bed like a blind snake and touched my shoulder. I tried to hold still because I knew that if I moved, the rat would know where I was hiding. I turned my face away and squeezed my eyes shut. I held my breath. I tried to hold still while the smelly pink tail slithered over my chest and up toward my face, but I couldn't. I shrank away from it, and in a second the huge nose was sniffing under the bed for me.

I scrambled to the far side of the bed. The rat was too big to fit in the space beneath the box spring, but it forced its long snout under and sniffed at me. I could hear its long whiskers scraping the bed frame. I could smell its rancid, hot breath.

After a moment, the nose withdrew. A second later I heard something smash to the floor. The room suddenly plunged into darkness; the rat had knocked over my lamp!

I heard the bed springs groan suddenly as the huge rat bounded over the top of my bed to try to get to me on the other side. I scrambled across to the far side before the nose poked under again. The rat snarled.

How long can this go on? I wondered. I yelled for help, but I knew my voice was muffled by the bed. No help came. The rat hissed and snarled, furious that it couldn't reach me.

I heard a creaking noise and felt the bed lift suddenly away from my face. The rat was tipping up my bed. I scrambled toward the foot of the bed as the whole thing toppled over on its side, and then I heard the crash as the bed rolled completely over, smashing my dresser and the window.

I sprinted to the door and threw it open. I dashed to the top of the stairs screaming as I ran. I was bounding down three steps at a time when it hit me—I should have slammed the door behind me. By now I could hear the huge rat scuffling through my bedroom doorway, its claws ripping at the hallway carpet.

I ran through the dark kitchen and tried to open the back door. It was locked. I struggled to twist the stiff deadbolt, but it wouldn't budge. I heard claws scrabbling onto the kitchen floor tiles. The rat was right behind me.

I dove under the kitchen table and curled into a ball with my eyes squeezed shut. I heard the thudding footsteps of the rat as it trotted over to the table. I felt the kitchen floor vibrate with each step.

There was a loud clattering and splintering of wood as a kitchen chair skittered across the kitchen floor and smashed against the stove.

I kept my eyes closed tight as the rat's cold, wet nose sniffed me all over. I felt its hot breath on the back of my neck and its whiskers like quills trailing down my back. Its stench filled my nostrils.

A claw gripped my shoulder and pulled me over on my back. It pinned me to the floor. I screamed.

And then the rat screamed—like a woman.

I opened my eyes. Mom was looking down at me, holding one hand against her chest. I was lying in bed.

"You scared me to death," she said. "I'm just trying to wake you up for breakfast. You don't have to scream at me."

I was still shaking. "I was having a bad dream," I gasped. "It was terrible." I could feel beads of cold sweat on my forehead. My bedclothes were twisted around my legs. My body heaved with each breath I took.

Mom sat at the edge of my bed and smoothed down my damp hair with her hand. "It's all right now, honey," she said reassuringly. "Everything is OK."

I tried to smile up at her, but it was hard. Nothing was OK.

CHAPTER 10

Brad came over after breakfast, the way he had every day that week. He looked energetic and eager to work when I opened the front door. I wondered how I looked to him.

We walked through the house and out the kitchen door. I looked at all the junk that crowded the driveway, every piece of it organized in some strange arrangement known only to Andrea. Like using stepping stones to cross a river, we had to step carefully over boxes and vases and old typewriters to make our slow way to the garage.

When we got to the garage door, I stooped to lift it open, and then hefted it above my head. Brad stood for a moment peering into the garage.

"*There's* something I thought I'd never live to see," he said.

I looked, anxiously, to see what he was talking about. I saw a bunch of boxes, a hat stand, an old-fashioned bathtub, and a rusty telescope tripod. None of that looked unusual.

"What?" I asked him. "What did you think you'd never see?"

"The back of the garage," he said grinning.

I looked in again. It was true. In the bright light of morning, we could finally see the beams and tar paper of the garage's back wall through the junk that was left.

"It's Friday," Brad said. "We're actually going to get this done on time."

He held up his right hand, and I gave him a high five.

Now that we were so close to being done, the work seemed somehow easier. Andrea came out before long and began writing down prices for all the junk she was going to sell at the garage sale. Dad's pickup was almost filled up for the fourth time—he'd already made three trips to the dump after work earlier in the week. Brad carried things out of the garage, I cleaned them and Andrea sorted and priced them. We worked for nearly an hour in silence, each of us doing our separate jobs.

After the mailman came by, Andrea said we all needed a break and went inside to get us some lemonade. I dabbed the sweat from my eyes with the hem of my tee shirt and went back to cleaning a set of TV trays with a sponge and a bucket of sudsy water.

Brad carried a plump, canvas duffel bag from the garage and set it on the concrete. He squatted down and slapped a cloud of dust from it.

"Know what this is?" he asked.

I had no idea.

"It's a tent," he said. "It looks like a pretty big one. You think I could buy this at the garage sale? How much do you think it's going to cost?"

I dropped my sponge into the bucket of soapy water and looked at Brad. He was pulling the tent from the bag to see if it was still usable. His forehead was beaded with sweat. He'd worked hard all week helping us, but aside from the sandwiches Andrea made him, he'd gotten nothing in return. He didn't seem to expect anything, either. I felt kind of bad that I had no money to pay him, but if I *had* offered him money, I knew he wouldn't take it—he was that kind of guy.

I knew he had better things to do with his summer vacation than help me get my chores done. I wondered if *I* would have worked this hard to help him if this was his chore. It was an easy question to answer. I knew I wouldn't have.

"You want the tent?" I asked him. "It's yours."

He looked up suddenly with a surprised look on his face.

"You mean it?" he asked. "You could get some money for this at the garage sale."

"Take it," I said.

"Shouldn't you ask your dad?"

"Dad told Andrea she could decide what to do with anything we found in the garage," I said. "It's her call."

We both looked over at Andrea. She was coming up the driveway with a tray of lemonade glasses, trying to navigate a safe path through all the junk. I knew what she'd say. She would have given Brad our dad's pickup if he'd asked for it.

"Of course you can have it, Brad," she said. "You've earned it."

Brad looked at me and then back at Andrea. "Thanks, you guys," he said. "But I'd feel a lot better if you cleared it with your dad when he gets home."

"No sweat," I said. "I'll tell him. He won't mind. He knows how much you've helped us this week."

Brad spread the tent out on the lawn to check for tears and holes. It was fairly old, but it looked like it had never been used.

"We can put it up now to see if all the parts are there," I suggested.

"You think we have time?"

"Sure," I told him. "We don't have much left to do. We'll have the garage empty by this afternoon, easy."

We dragged the tent to the middle of the lawn and set it up while Andrea went around the driveway putting masking tape price tags on everything. All the parts of the tent were in the bag: the stakes, the poles, the ropes—everything. I watched Brad hammer a metal stake into the grass. He looked like he was really enjoying himself.

When we were done setting up the tent, I unzipped the door and we went inside. I sat down on the floor and let my eyes adjust to the semi-darkness. It smelled a little musty, but it felt cool after our morning in the summer sun. Pinpricks of light showed through the canvas here and there.

Brad checked all the tent seams for tears, and I lay on my back with my hands behind my head. I was trying to relax, but I kept thinking about the mess I was in.

"You OK?" Brad asked me. I hadn't realized he was watching me.

"I guess so."

"Are you sure?" he asked. "You seem kind of worried and distracted these last few days."

I sighed. I really wanted to tell him. But I didn't know how to begin.

"What is it?" he asked. "You don't have to tell me if you don't want to, but maybe I can help."

Brad was a good friend. He wasn't like a lot of other kids I knew at school, who were always looking for somebody to make fun of. I knew I could trust him.

"Ever do something dumb and it keeps getting bigger and bigger until you can't stop it anymore?" I asked him.

"Yeah," Brad admitted. "I remember once I told a lie to my teacher, and I kept having to lie more and more to cover up the first lie. It was awful."

"This is bigger," I said. "Someone might get hurt."

Brad sat down next to me. "Are you in some kind of trouble?" he asked.

"Yeah," I said. "Big trouble. You wouldn't believe me if I told you."

"Try me," he said. "Tell me about it. Maybe there's something I can do to help."

I really wanted to tell him, but I couldn't think of how to say it without sounding like a complete idiot. Brad wouldn't make fun of me, but even *he* wouldn't believe me.

"How about if I *show* you?" I said. "You're not going to believe it any other way. You've got to see it with your own two eyes."

"Sure," he said. "OK."

"Tonight," I told him. "I'll show you tonight. Think your dad would let you sleep out here in the tent with me?"

"Sure," he shrugged. "I guess so."

I thought for a minute.

"Bring your pellet gun," I told him. "Just in case."

CHAPTER 11

We unrolled our sleeping bags inside the tent while there was still some daylight. The green canvas tent panels glowed on the side facing the setting sun. I could feel a few lumpy spots of grass under the tent floor. The tent was tall enough that we could stand up inside without stooping.

Brad brought a small flashlight with him. I had four other flashlights and a battery lantern, just in case. I sat down on my sleeping bag.

"What do we need with all this stuff?" Brad asked, standing over me and looking around the floor of the tent at my assortment of lights and other equipment. "Baseball bats?" he said. "An archery set? All these flashlights? My pellet gun? Have you invented some new kind of indoor sport?"

"You'll see," I promised him.

He looked at me for a moment in the growing darkness, and then something seemed to occur to him. "Is all this stuff to protect ourselves from something?" he asked.

I didn't want to scare him off, but I had to tell the truth. I nodded.

Brad looked suddenly nervous. "Just what is it you're going to show me?" he asked.

"Promise you'll stay here, even if what I tell you sounds crazy?"

Brad stood there, thinking. I knew it was a hard promise to make. He had no idea what I might tell him, and he wasn't the kind of guy who would break a promise. "Sure," he said after a minute. "I guess so."

Brad sat down in front of me and leaned in close. It was getting dark inside the tent, so I switched on the battery lantern and set it between us on the floor of the tent. It glowed like a campfire.

"OK," Brad said. "Let's hear it."

"You promise you won't say anything until I'm done with my story?"

"Yeah," he said. "I promise."

I took a deep breath and plunged into my story. "All right," I said. "A few days ago I accidentally created a giant, mutant rat." I held up my hand to remind him that he wasn't supposed to talk. I told him the whole story.

When I had told him everything, Brad looked at me a long time in silence. His face was bright in the yellow light of the lantern, but the rest of the tent was in shadows. A breeze flapped the wall of the tent behind him. I waited for him to say something.

"Well?" I said after a moment. "You think I've completely lost my mind, or what?"

Brad shook his head. He looked real serious. "This is God's world," he told me. "Nothing is impossible." The lantern cast a large shadow of Brad on the wall of the tent behind him. "I believe in a lot of things other people think are crazy," he said. "I believe God created a monster fish to swallow Jonah. I believe God created the whole world in six days. Everything is possible because God is real."

"So you actually believe me? You don't think I'm nuts?"

"I don't know if there is a monster rat out there eating poodles," he said. "But I do know that there *could* be, if God wanted it."

I knew what he was saying, but it didn't make a whole lot of sense to me right then. "OK," I said.

"But why would God *want* there to be a monster rat out there?"

"I don't know," Brad admitted, shrugging his shoulders. "That's God's business. But part of it might be that he's trying to teach you something."

"Yeah right," I said. "Like God's going to waste his time doing all this to try to teach *me* something. He's God. I'm sure he's got more important things to do."

Brad shook his head. "You *are* important to God," he told me. "God loves you. Christ died on the cross for you—*that's* how much he loves you."

It still didn't make much sense to me. "If he loves me so much, how come he let me get myself in such a mess?" I asked.

"You said it yourself," Brad told me. "*Who* got you into this mess?"

"*I* did," I admitted.

"Right," Brad said. "If you'd obeyed your dad and hadn't tried to hide the broken chemistry set from him, none of this would have happened, would it? That's why God gives us these rules to live by. They're for our own good."

He was right. I couldn't argue with him.

"Here's the good news," Brad said. "God's always willing to help you when you get in trouble. All you have to do is ask him."

I didn't say anything. What he was saying was nice to think about, but it was hard to believe. I stared at the glowing lantern on the ground in front of me.

How could God love me so much? I was just a dumb kid. I'd done a lot of bad things—more than I could even remember. I didn't feel lovable. Even my family was mad at me half the time, and they *had* to love me.

Brad was watching me. I guess he knew what I was thinking.

"Think about it," Brad said. "Both of us are going to be in a lot of tough situations in our lives. Me? I don't want to face them by myself."

I guess that was what Brad meant when he told me that he never feels alone. He always had someone on his side, someone watching over him. I wished *I* had that kind of assurance.

I lay down on my sleeping bag and put my hands behind my head. I looked up at the roof of the tent. Brad had given me a lot to think about, but I felt too exhausted to figure it all out right then.

CHAPTER 12

Brad was lying on his back on top of his sleeping bag reading his Bible when it occurred to me that the crickets outside had stopped their chirping. I lay still for a moment, listening. The crickets in the yard stayed silent.

"The light," I whispered. "Turn off the light."

Brad reached behind him and switched off the lantern. In the sudden darkness I could hear Brad sit up. I felt around me for a baseball bat. Last night's nightmare was fresh in my mind—like it had *really* happened.

"Is it here?" Brad whispered.

"I don't know," I said. "I think so."

I could hear Brad pick up his pellet gun and pump it a few times. My eyes began to adjust to the darkness, and in a moment I could make out Brad's shape, sitting up on his sleeping bag with the pellet gun across his lap. He was facing the front of the tent. I turned and began warily to watch the door of the tent.

The porch light behind Mrs. Petersen's house cast a shadow of our backyard wall in a straight line across a side panel of the tent. I could hear Brad's nervous breathing.

"You scared?" I asked him.

"Yeah," he whispered back. "You?"

"Terrified," I admitted.

I thought about Brad's pellet gun and the baseball bat I was clutching in both hands. Would they really be of any use against the kind of monster in my nightmare? "You think God will protect us?" I asked Brad.

"He can," Brad said. "Ever hear of Daniel in the lion's den?"

"Yeah," I said. "Now we've got Daniel in the rat's yard."

I could tell Brad was grinning in the darkness.

"You think *that* Daniel was nervous?" I asked him.

"Probably not as much as I am now," he said.

Just then a giant shadow fell across the side of the tent. I gasped. Brad spun around to see what I was looking at. The shadow crept slowly along the dark line cast by the backyard wall, with a huge, narrow nose twitching in the air, and pointy ears as big as my hands. Suddenly Brad was beside me. I could feel him shaking. Or maybe I was shaking against him. We both scooted backward until we were pressed against the far side of the tent. I gripped the handle of my baseball bat, ready to swing. Brad pumped his pellet gun a few more times. The huge shadow kept moving slowly across the side of the tent.

"It's crawling along the back wall," I whispered. "I've seen it do that from my window."

The shadow looked as big as Mom's station wagon. The twitching nose disappeared and, for a moment, the rat's body blotted out Mrs. Petersen's porch light completely. The rat's shadow almost completely filled the side panel of the tent. I bit my lip. My stomach was twisted in knots.

Then came the huge slope of the rat's haunches and the shadow of its long pointed tail. The tail dragged along behind like a fat boa constrictor slowly curling and writhing.

The rat seemed to take forever to creep past, but finally the tip of its tail disappeared, and the garden wall cast a straight line of shadow across the side of the tent again.

"Believe me now?" I whispered, once I remembered to breathe.

"Yeah," Brad croaked. "I believe you."

We sat for a moment in the dark tent, straining to hear where the monster was now. The only sound was the wind in the trees.

"I don't know about you," I whispered. "But I'm not too thrilled with sleeping out in a tent tonight. I'd much rather be in my bedroom—with all the doors and windows locked."

"I'm with you," Brad said. "But how do we get to your back door? How do we know where Freddie the Giant Rat is? What if he's waiting for us in the yard somewhere?"

"Keep quiet and listen," I said.

Brad fell silent. "I don't hear anything," he said a minute later.

"Yes, you do," I told him.

He fell silent again for a few seconds. "Hey!" he said. "Crickets!"

The crickets had taken up their rhythmic chirping again. It seemed like a good sign to me. I crawled to the tent door on my elbows with my flashlight and baseball bat. I let go of the baseball bat and tugged the zipper up a few inches. I peeked out. I could dimly see the top half of our house in the light from Mrs. Petersen's back porch light. Nothing moved in the dark yard.

I pulled the zipper up a few more inches and shone the flashlight around the yard. I didn't see anything move. I looked back at Brad. He was holding his pellet gun pointed at the roof of the tent.

"Let's go," I said. "We'll walk back-to-back, so nothing can sneak up on us."

I grabbed the baseball bat again, crawled from the tent, and slowly stood up. The crickets stopped chirping again. I hoped it was because of *me*. I held the baseball bat in the air like a club with one hand and pointed a shaky flashlight beam around the yard with the other. Brad wriggled out and stood up behind me. He switched on his own flashlight.

"You face the house," he told me. "You lead the way. I'll cover the yard with my pellet gun."

The beams of our flashlights scoured the yard as we inched our way toward the door. Our backs were pressed so tightly together we must have looked like some kind of monster ourselves—a monster with four legs and two glowing eyes scanning the yard.

We made it over Mom's flower bed to the driveway and then we had to move even more slowly. I led us along a winding path through all the stuff Andrea had arranged on the back drive for the garage sale. As the beams of our flashlights moved across the junk, strangely shaped shadows seemed to creep spookily behind them. We inched around a tall hat stand and threaded our way between some boxes of baby toys. We had only to edge our way around an old bathtub full of gardening tools now to reach the door.

"Almost there," I whispered.

In a few seconds we were so close to the kitchen door I felt like cheering.

As I stepped around the old claw-footed bathtub, something streaked out from underneath. I yelled and swung my bat wildly, smashing an already broken table lamp.

The Jacobs's cat let out a yowl and leaped over the side fence into Brad's yard. I tripped backwards over a footstool and knocked Brad down. I tumbled on top of him, and his pellet gun poked me in the back. I started to giggle.

"Owww," Brad said. "What happened?"

I helped him up, but I couldn't stop laughing—even though I was scared to death.

"What happened?" Brad asked again as I pushed him through the back door and pushed it shut behind us.

"It was just a cat," I told him as I bolted the door.

"A giant, mutant cat?" he asked.

I started laughing again. I felt relieved and giddy knowing we were safe inside the house now.

"No," I said. "It was just the Jacobs's cat again. I hope it gets home before it becomes rat food."

CHAPTER 13

The next morning was Saturday. While Mom, Dad, and Andrea were busy running the garage sale out front, Brad and I loaded up the last truckload of junk in the back of Dad's pickup so it could be taken to the dump. It was hot, dusty work, but it felt good to see this nightmare of a chore so close to being finished. I could relax a while, because I knew the rat was curled up somewhere, asleep.

Andrea was keeping herself busy up front. Every time I glanced over the driveway fence into the front yard it seemed like a new car was pulling up to take a look at the garage sale. Andrea ran up to each car like some kind of hostess and welcomed each new arrival to her sale. She must have been selling a lot of stuff, because every few minutes I heard a car's trunk slamming shut.

At about eleven o'clock, I went into the kitchen to get a couple of cans of soda for Brad and myself. When I came back outside, Brad was leaning on a broom and looking down at the old claw-footed bathtub. He appeared deep in thought.

"What's up?" I asked, handing him a lemon-lime soda.

He didn't say anything. He just popped open the can of soda and took a long sip. He wiped his brow with his wrist and took another sip.

"I think I've got an idea," he said at last, gesturing down at the old tub with his can of soda. "If we could *capture* Freddie the Giant Rat, everyone would see it and they'd have to believe our story," he said. "No one would get hurt, and we wouldn't even have to hurt the monster rat—he'd probably end up in a zoo or something. All our problems would be taken care of."

"Yeah, OK," I said. "But how do you go about capturing a giant, mutant rat in the first place?"

"With this," he said, tapping the side of the bathtub with the toe of one of his sneakers.

In a few minutes, we'd emptied out the tub and dragged it over near the back wall. We rolled it over so that the clawed feet were sticking up in the air. Lying on its back, it looked like a dead cow or something.

We propped up one end with a wooden orange crate and tied a long rope to the crate. Brad found some harness bells in a box of old Christmas decorations we'd packed in the back of Dad's pickup, and he tied long strings to them. He taped the strings inside the bathtub so that the bells hung down a few inches off the lawn.

If the rat went under the bathtub at night, we'd hear the bells ring. That would be our signal to pull out the orange crate with the rope, trapping the giant rat under the bathtub—*if* he hadn't grown too big. It was hard to know how big he might have grown on his steady diet of poodles and cats.

To be on the safe side, we stacked some weights from Brad's weightlifting set next to the tub. Once Freddie the Giant Rat was trapped inside, we would pile the weights on top of the tub—just to make extra sure that he couldn't get out.

The whole time we worked, we could hear voices and laughter and car doors slamming out in front of the house. It was weird to think that none of the people coming to the garage sale knew that Brad and I were working to make their neighborhood safe again. None of them knew what danger they'd been in for the last week. But if our plan worked, soon they'd all know about Freddie the

Giant Rat!

Once the trap was ready, we covered it with a tarp. Then we took down the tent and turned it so that the door was facing the trap.

All we needed now was some bait.

That afternoon, Brad went home and I went out front to help with the garage sale. Mom, Dad, and Andrea were all so busy, none of them noticed the weird shape under the tarp in the backyard. There was a steady stream of customers until well after our usual dinner time. When the last customers left, there wasn't much of anything left out on the front lawn. Dad said we could just add it to the junk in the back of the pickup.

We ordered take-out pizza for dinner so Mom wouldn't have to cook. I can usually eat a whole pizza by myself, but tonight I barely ate one piece. I was too nervous and excited thinking about what would happen after the sun went down.

After dinner, I took a couple of slices of pepperoni pizza and some chicken scraps out of the refrigerator and wrapped them in foil. I added half a baked potato, some carrots, and a stale hot dog bun. I figured that rats ate just about anything, and a giant, mutant rat was probably no more picky than a regular one. But what if the rat had already eaten? What if Freddie had already come across a sleeping Chihuahua?

I was about to shut the refrigerator door when I noticed the cheesecake. Mice like cheese, so cheesecake might be just the thing a giant rat would crave for dessert after a dinner of cocker spaniel or Siamese cat. I added two slices of cake to the food I'd already collected and then wrapped the foil tight.

When the sun went down and the streetlights out front began to flicker on, I took the foil-wrapped bait and went out to the backyard. I went around the side of the house and called up to Brad's bedroom window. He came to the window and gave me the thumbs-up sign, and in a few minutes he came out his own kitchen door with his pellet gun, flashlight, and a brown paper bag.

Neither of our parents seemed surprised that we wanted to camp out again; they thought we were simply having some harmless fun in the backyard in Brad's new tent.

Brad handed his paper bag of leftovers over the fence, and then he passed his pellet gun over. He gave me his flashlight last and climbed over into my yard.

I shone my flashlight into Brad's paper bag. He had two cold slices of meatloaf, some graham crackers, and an apple.

"Rats don't eat fruit, do they?" I asked.

"The apple's for me," he told me. "I'm still hungry."

We pulled the tarp off the bathtub trap, careful not to set the harness bells jingling and draw any attention to what we were doing. Brad held the flashlight for me while I spread the foil on the grass beneath the bathtub and arranged all the scraps of food on it—a complete rat picnic. Every time my hand brushed against one of the bells, it tinkled quietly. Nothing could get under that bathtub without our hearing it!

I dragged the rope along the grass and tossed the free end in through the door of the tent. Both of us crawled in after it. Inside, I pulled the rope taut. One good tug on the rope and the bathtub would fall. I zipped the tent door closed.

Brad left his pellet gun at the front of the tent and stretched out on his sleeping bag. He had his brother's glow-in-the dark watch with him tonight.

"Nine-fifteen," he said. "We've probably got a few hours before Freddie shows up. What should we do?"

"Let's talk," I told him. "I've been thinking a lot about those things you said last night—about God and stuff."

"Yeah?" Brad said. "That's good to hear."

"If we survive this—I mean if we're both still alive in the morning—you think I could go to Sunday school with you tomorrow?"

I could see Brad raise himself up on his elbows in the shadows. "Sure!" he said. He sounded genuinely excited. "My family would love to have you come along. And there's plenty of room in the van. Just make sure it's OK with your folks."

CHAPTER 14

When I first woke up, I didn't know where I was or what had wakened me. I thought I was in my bedroom—but I could hear a harp playing somewhere. I opened my eyes, and it all came back to me. It wasn't a harp—it was the harness bells jingling in our trap.

I sat up and looked around in the dark. Brad was already kneeling, holding the rope. He'd wrapped it around his hand a few times. He was ready to give it a good yank. My hand moved around the floor of the tent until I found the flashlight and pulled it close.

"It just started," Brad whispered. "I want to make sure he's all the way under the tub before I pull out the orange crate."

We listened. The bells continued to tinkle quietly, then we heard the sound of crumpling foil.

"Here goes," Brad said.

I held my breath.

Brad yanked hard, and we felt the heavy bathtub hit the ground outside the tent with a thump.

I scrambled to the door of the tent with my flashlight. Brad snatched up the pellet gun and crawled up next to me.

"Ready?" I asked him.

"Yeah," he whispered breathlessly.

I tugged the zipper on the front flap as high as I could. Brad poked the end of his gun out, and I shone my flashlight over his shoulder.

The bathtub was lying flat on the ground now. I scanned the yard with the light. I shone it over the wall and the lawn, the bushes and Mom's flower beds. Nothing moved. It looked safe. We crawled out of the tent onto the damp lawn.

The two of us crept up on the bathtub. Brad kept his gun trained on it the whole time and I kept it lit with my flashlight. As we came closer, we could hear something clanging around inside and the mad, faint jingling of bells. Freddie the Giant Rat sounded angry, but he was definitely trapped under the tub.

Brad jumped up and sat on the bathtub until I

could stack the weights on top, then he jumped down again and we both backed away. I felt thrilled and relieved. I felt like doing a jig right there and then.

"Whoo-hoo," I shouted with my fist in the air.

"Freddie the Rat is in the bathtub!" Brad shouted and gave me a high five.

"He's all washed up!" I said. We laughed and danced around like crazy men.

A light came on inside our house. We couldn't stop laughing. A minute later, I saw Dad cup his hands against the window upstairs and peer down at us. His window slid open.

"What's going on down there?" he called in a whispery kind of shout. He sounded angry and sleepy. I shone my flashlight up at him.

"Get that thing out of my face," he yelled, trying to keep his voice low.

I pointed my flashlight at the ground.

"What's all this racket?" Dad demanded. "What are the two of you doing down there?"

I pointed the flashlight at my own face so he could see me. "It's a monster!" I called up to him, blinking in the bright light. "We trapped a giant, mutant rat!"

The yard was silent for a few seconds. I couldn't

see Dad anymore, so I pointed the light down at the lawn. "What on earth are you talking about?" Dad demanded.

"It's true," I said. "We can prove it now. We trapped it under the bathtub." I shone the light at the upside-down bathtub behind us. *"See?"*

A light came on in Brad's house and one in the Jacobs's house. A dog began to bark nearby.

"Keep your voice down," Dad called down at me. "You're waking up the whole neighborhood."

A light came on in Mrs. Petersen's house. A window slid open somewhere.

"You don't understand," I insisted. "We've got a big ol' monster rat trapped down here. It's got to be eight feet long by now. We need some help. You should call the police or something."

Dad was silent a minute. "I don't get it," he said. "What are you boys up to?"

"Daniel's telling the truth," Brad offered. I shone the flashlight in his face, but he waved it away. "We trapped a giant rat down here."

I saw the light go on in Andrea's room. Dad said something over his shoulder to Mom.

"OK," Dad called down. "I'll be out in a second. Just keep it down."

The bathtub behind us began to shake suddenly. One of the weights slipped off and thudded to the lawn. Brad and I both backed farther away.

"Hurry!" I yelled.

"What's going on over there?" an angry voice called. It was Mr. Jacobs, standing in his back door.

CHAPTER 15

In five minutes there were more than a dozen of us milling around in the backyard. Most of the neighbors were wearing bathrobes, but a few were fully dressed or had at least pulled on a sweat suit before leaving their houses. A couple of the women had curlers in their hair. None of them were very happy.

Although they all insisted that what Brad and I were saying was *impossible,* most of them had brought along rakes or golf clubs or bats to defend themselves—and no one would go anywhere near the upside-down bathtub. Mr. Jacobs called the police from his house.

Andrea came to the kitchen door in her bathrobe and slippers. She leaned out the back door to see what was going on and then switched on the back porch light. It hadn't occurred to any of the rest of us. I switched off my flashlight.

Andrea came down the back steps. She was the last one to join the group. I could tell she'd stopped to brush her hair, since she knew Brad was out here. She'd probably brushed her teeth as well.

"What's going on out here?" she asked me.

"We trapped a ten-foot-long rat!" I said, still tingling with excitement. "Brad and I have captured the monster rat that has been prowling the neighborhood."

She looked from me to Brad and then back at me.

"Have you lost your mind?" she said directly to me. Brad didn't seem to be included in the question. "Ten feet long? That's impossible."

"No, Miss Smarty-Pants," I said laughing. "For the first time ever, *I'm* right and *you're* wrong. There's a giant rat under that bathtub over there. It's been prowling around every night eating neighborhood pets. *That's* what happened to Truman the poodle. Freddie the Rat ate him."

Andrea laughed. "Truman came home last night," she said. "Mrs. Petersen had him with her when she came by the garage sale this morning." She looked at the back wall. "That's Truman barking now."

I stopped for a minute to catch my breath and heard Truman's familiar yapping on the other side of the wall. I looked at Andrea, blinking. "But, how—?"

Just then, flashing lights lit up the garage. The police had arrived. I could hear the loud voice of a woman saying numbers on the police radio in front of the house. I heard two car doors slam. If any of our neighbors had been still asleep, they weren't now.

In a few seconds, two policemen came through the side gate. One of them was very tall. They seemed surprised to see so many people milling around in our yard in the middle of the night carrying rakes and brooms.

"Who lives here?" the shorter policeman demanded.

Everyone looked at Dad. He raised his hand like a kid who had just been caught throwing spit wads in school. He looked more than a little nervous.

"What's the trouble here, sir?" the shorter policeman asked. "What's this all about?"

Dad glanced over at me. It was clear he didn't know where to begin. "These boys say they've trapped some kind of monster rat under that bathtub over there." Dad pointed toward the shadowy back wall where the porch light didn't quite reach. "And there *is* something under there. You can hear it moving around."

Both policemen looked at the dimly lit bathtub and then looked at me and Brad. They didn't look pleased.

"What's going on here, boys?" the tall one said. "What are you two up to?"

I looked at Brad. He had his pellet gun slung over his shoulder. He shrugged. Everyone seemed to move closer around us. None of the neighbors wanted to look like they were listening, but it was clear that no one wanted to miss a word.

"We trapped it," I said to the policeman.

"Trapped what, son?" the shorter one asked.

"A giant, mutant rat," I offered.

"It's ten feet long," Andrea added. I knew she didn't believe that—she was just saying it to tease me.

The policemen looked at each other and then back at me.

"You're saying there's a ten-foot-long, mutant rat under that bathtub over there?" the tall policeman asked. He started to laugh.

"It's *true,*" I insisted. "I've seen it with my own eyes."

Brad backed me up. "*I* saw its shadow on the

tent last night."

"We call it Freddie," I added, and then wished I hadn't.

The tall police officer looked around the yard. He took off his cap and scratched his head. "What do we do now, Sarge?" he asked.

"I don't know," the other laughed. "Twenty-three years on the force, and this is my first giant, mutant rat call."

Everyone looked at the bathtub in silence for a moment.

"Maybe you should call for backup," I suggested.

The sergeant looked at me and snorted, "Kid, you're outta your mind. There's no such thing as a giant, mutant rat. It's probably a rabbit or something."

"Let's do it, Sarge," the tall policeman said. He seemed oddly excited. "Let's turn the thing over and see what's inside."

"I suppose we should," the sergeant said. "It may be the only way we can get these folks to go back to bed."

The policemen made everyone back away from the tub, and then they got out their guns. They slowly walked up to the bathtub. The taller one walked around the tub once, studying it, and then tapped the side with his boot, like he was kicking the tires of a used car. He shrugged and the two of them went into a huddle. The sergeant kept glancing over at the rest of us as they whispered together. None of us could hear what they were saying.

Now that they'd told everyone they were going to see what was trapped under the tub, they didn't seem to be in any hurry to get the job done; they just stood there whispering back and forth. It seemed like they might have been arguing about who should be the one to lift up the bathtub.

Finally the sergeant backed away and pointed his flashlight and gun at the tub. The tall policeman cleared the weights off the top and then stopped and looked at everyone watching him. He looked like he was nervous but didn't want anyone to know. He cracked his knuckles and shook out his arms like he was about to lift a barbell. Then he squatted down and got a grip on the edge of the tub.

Everyone in the yard backed farther away. Mom pulled me close to her.

The policeman grunted and lifted the tub. Harness bells jingled.

Everyone gasped when they saw how big the rat was.

And then, suddenly, everyone started laughing.

The sergeant laughed so hard he dropped his flashlight. The other policeman pulled the tub clear and dropped it on the lawn. He slapped imaginary dust off his hands and grinned at me from the shadows.

The giant rat lay perfectly still, tangled in string and harness bells. It looked like it was dead. It wasn't ten feet long, but it *was* big. It was definitely nothing to laugh at.

I looked around at everyone. They were still laughing hysterically. Andrea and Brad were laughing now too.

"What's so funny?" I demanded. "Why is everyone laughing?"

No one answered. No one could stop laughing long enough. A couple of neighbors headed out the side gate dragging their rakes behind them and shaking their heads. They were still laughing as they pulled the gate closed behind them.

After a while the laughter began to die down. Mr. Jacobs, still chuckling, took off his glasses and dabbed tears from his eyes with the sleeve of his bathrobe. I'd never seem him laugh so hard.

I looked around at everyone, confused.

"That's the biggest possum I've ever seen," the sergeant said. "Maybe we *should* call for backup."

Everyone started roaring again.

"Possum?" I said. "Freddie's an opossum?"

Mom bent down and hugged me. Dad patted my head. It took a minute, but soon I began to laugh too.

When the neighbors were finally gone and we were safely back in the house, I told Dad everything. The two of us sat at the kitchen table, and I gave him the whole story, starting with the chemistry set and ending when he came to the window. I didn't leave anything out.

It felt good to get it off my chest at last.

CHAPTER 16

It was hard to get up in the morning after being up so late, but it was something I really wanted to do. I made sure my radio alarm was turned up loud.

I washed my face and brushed my teeth and chose a nice shirt and a pair of pants.

I fixed my own breakfast and ate it alone at the kitchen table. When I was done, I looked at the clock and went out to the living room.

Andrea was sitting on the sofa buckling her shiny black shoe. She was wearing her white, frilly dress again and her hat with the cloth flowers on it.

"What are *you* doing up so early?" I asked her.

"I'm coming too," she said. "Mom and Dad said it was OK."

"You're going to Sunday school? You realize this kind of school doesn't involve math, don't you?" I teased her.

She made a face and stood up, brushing down her dress with both hands.

"Do I look OK?" she asked spinning in a circle like a fashion model.

I laughed. "Brad will be very impressed," I told her.

I opened the front door, and the two of us walked over to Brad's house. Brad's family was getting into their van. When Brad saw us he waved us over. He looked happy and excited to see us.

"I was hoping you'd both come," he called to us across the lawn.

Andrea leaned in close to me. "Dibs on the seat next to Brad," she whispered as we walked across Brad's front yard. I laughed and put my arm around her shoulder.

"It's yours," I told her.

The End

Don't miss another exciting

HEEBIE JEEBIES

adventure!

Turn the page to check out a chapter from

WELCOME TO CAMP CREEPS

Welcome to Camp Creeps

Chapter 1

Pine needles snapped under my feet as I stumbled through the dark night. My little brother, Todd, had just swiped my flashlight and run ahead before I could get it back. That he got away from me wasn't just annoying, it was amazing. Normally he moves like a barge. With his thick ankles and pudgy frame, he's anything but fast.

"Wait!" I shouted, glancing from side to side. I had never been in these woods before and wasn't about to be stranded alone. Talk about creep central! The trees looked alive, like they were following me.

"Forget you, Heather the Feather," Todd yelled over his shoulder.

That did it! I was tired of Todd making fun of my weight. Or, more precisely, my lack of it. My *real* name is Heather Marie Pierce. I have reddish-blond hair, and twenty-three freckles on each cheek (if you want to get technical, it's actually twenty-six and twenty-eight, but in my opinion some are too small to count). Sure, I'm kind of skinny. But I'm thirteen and Todd's only eleven. I'm also taller than he is, which means I'm still his *big* sister.

I started to run as fast as I could, determined to catch the little pest. He would be sorry this time.

The wind howled through the branches above as I jumped rocks and ducked under branches. The twigs I couldn't dodge, I pushed out of the way. *Nothing to it,* I thought.

Wham! I plowed right into a tree and fell to the ground.

"Where did that come from?" I murmured.

Rubbing the lump on my forehead, sticky with sap, I sat there in a daze. Everything seemed blurry. Then an eerie sound caught my attention. Pine needles crunched nearby. Something was coming! Suddenly two pale yellow lights came into focus. They inched through the shadows, closer.

I waved my hand and was greeted by a vicious growl. Whoever or *whatever* was behind those eyes was *not* in a good mood.

"Todd?" I yelled. No response. I strained my eyes to look down the trail. More darkness.

The fiery eyes pushed forward, crunching the matted earth with each step. Two rows of razor-sharp, white teeth flashed in the night. The beast grumbled with hunger. *Grrrrr.*

Scrambling to my feet, I took off again. I sprinted as fast as I could. Dead branches scraped at my skin like claws, but I kept going. The trail widened. Glancing back, I couldn't see a thing. *Where was it? What was it?* I kept running, not wanting to find out.

"Todd!" I shouted, determined to track him down. "Get back here right now!"

The growls stopped. Was the beast running ahead to cut me off?

I could see my flashlight up ahead. Todd must have gotten scared and waited for me. Not that I blamed him.

Keep running, I told myself. *Ignore the sideache.* The flashlight was just ahead. But it wasn't moving. It was perfectly still. Another fifty feet and I'd be there.

I was breathing hard. Closing in. The flashlight still hadn't moved. What happened? How could Todd hold so still? And why wasn't he answering?

Twenty more feet. Almost there.

"Todd?" I screamed.

I stopped in horror. The light stood straight up in the center of the trail.

Todd was nowhere to be found.

More exciting releases from

THE NEW QUICK-READING TALES THAT ENTERTAIN WHILE AFFIRMING THE PRESENCE AND POWER OF GOD!

Heather and Todd are on a family vacation in the mountains when they stumble upon a mysterious abandoned camp ground. Wolves and spiders threaten the kids, but it's only when a phantom suddenly appears and begins to chase them that they fully understand the danger of their situation. In this eerie story filled with unexpected thrills and chills, Heather and Todd pursue an investigation to learn about the haunted camp, their father's own secret involvement, and God's all-powerful protection and love.

Welcome To Camp Creeps 0-8054-1195-X